THIS CANDLEWICK BOOK BELONGS TO:

_____

_____

_____

_____

For
Janet

All rights reserved.   First U.S. paperback edition 1997

The Library of Congress has cataloged the hardcover edition as follows:

McNaughton, Colin.
Here come the aliens! / Colin McNaughton.—1st U.S. ed.
Summary: A group of not-so-nice aliens speed toward Earth
looking for a fight—until something terrible scares them away.
ISBN 1-56402-642-6 (hardcover)
[1. Extraterrestrial beings—Fiction. 2. Humorous stories.
3. Stories in rhyme.] I. Title.
PZ8.3.M239He   1995   [E]—dc20   94-48912

ISBN 0-7636-0295-7 (paperback)

2 4 6 8 10 9 7 5 3 1

Printed in Hong Kong

This book was typeset in Kosmik.
The pictures were done in watercolor.

Candlewick Press, 2067 Massachusetts Avenue
Cambridge, Massachusetts 02140

In outer space
It's black as night
And something's moving—
Speed of light—
Something looking
for a fight ...

HERE COME
THE ALIENS!

Colin McNaughton

CANDLEWICK PRESS
CAMBRIDGE, MASSACHUSETTS

A fleet of spaceships heads this way.
They're fifty zillion miles away
But getting closer every day —
The aliens are coming!

They're zooming in from outer space
To conquer us, the human race.
We'll soon be standing face to face—
The aliens are coming!

The admiral's a fearsome sight—
A simple creature, not too bright;
All he wants to do is FIGHT!
The aliens are coming!

The first mate looks like wobbly jelly,
He's sort of gaseous and he's smelly;
He has an eyeball on his belly!
The aliens are coming!

These beings come in different sizes—
This one's doing exercises.
Get ready, Earth, for some surprises—
The aliens are coming!

Some have one head—some have two.
(There's even one with none, it's true!)
What on earth are we to do?
The aliens are coming!

They come from planets near and far—
Some big, some small, some quite bizarre.

Twinkle twinkle, little star —
The aliens are coming!

I really hate to make a fuss
.(Perhaps you thought they'd look like us),
But most of them appear thus.
The aliens are coming!

This one squeaks and that one squawks;
Some have eyeballs stuck on stalks.
This one squelches when it walks.
The aliens are coming!

See the aliens at lunch:
Slobber, dribble, gobble, munch.
Table manners? Not this bunch.
The aliens are coming!

Some are bald and some are hairy,
Some are roundy—some are squary.
Some look friendly but beware—
The aliens are coming!

They've boldly been where we've not been;
They're blue and purple, sickly green.
(At home this one's a beauty queen!)
The aliens are coming!

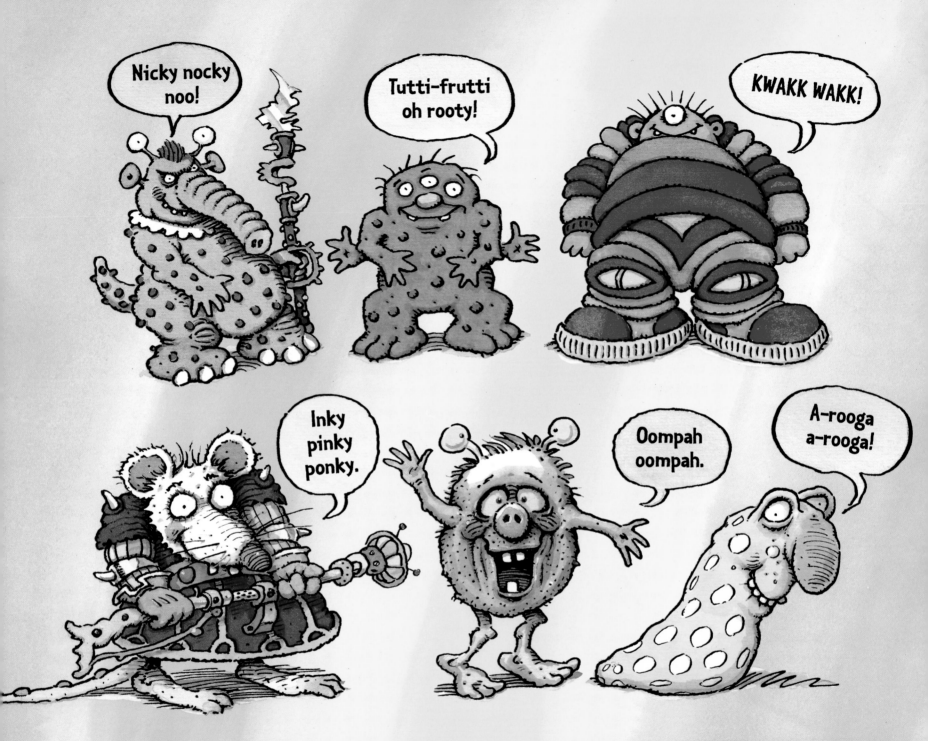

None speak English, French, or Greek.
They sort of grunt and burp and squeak.

The chance of peace talks? I'd say BLEAK!
The aliens are coming!

This one biffs and that one bops,
This one nips and that one chops.
Someone better call the cops!
The aliens are coming!

Some are tall and some are squat,
Some are cool and some are hot.
Some are nice but most are not!
The aliens are coming!

At last the earth comes into view.
The admiral knows what to do.
He orders, "BATTLE STATIONS, CREW!"
The aliens are coming!
BUT!
Approaching planet Earth, they see
(Though how it got there—don't ask me)
A piece of paper, floating free.
The aliens are slowing!

It's swiftly passed around the fleet.
A thousand hearts stop—miss a beat.
The order goes out: "FLEET RETREAT!!!"
The aliens are going!

For this is what the aliens saw:
A picture of you kids—aged four!

It's scared them off—away they roar.
The aliens are going!

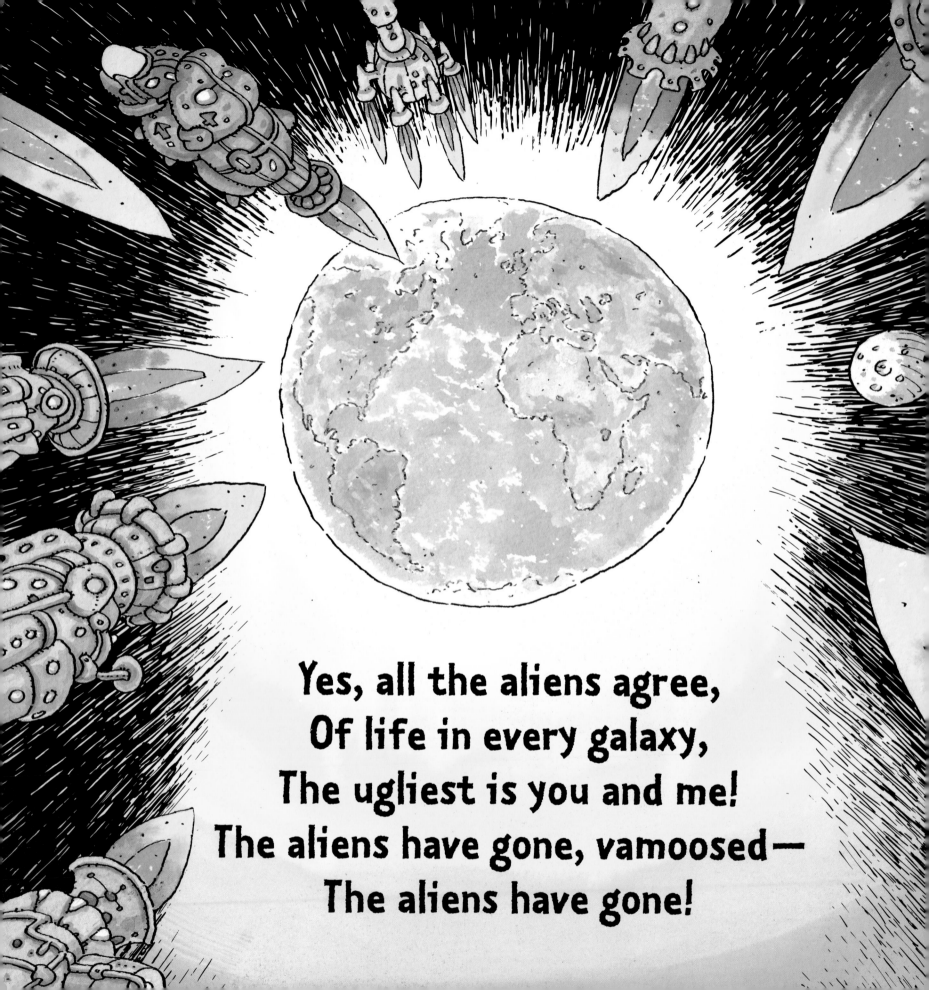

Yes, all the aliens agree,
Of life in every galaxy,
The ugliest is you and me!
The aliens have gone, vamoosed—
The aliens have gone!

Colin McNaughton has been drawing pirates and giants, monsters and aliens, since he was a boy, and all of them are lively, rambunctious characters that sing and talk and dance their way across the pages of his books. He admits that "the older I get the more I realize that my sense of humor is exactly the same as it was when I was four years old—it hasn't changed at all!" Of the fleet of "weird extraterrestrials" in *Here Come the Aliens!*, he says, "They're really just pirates in space."